I Think I Can

You Can Do It!

I0901380

Leonard Clasky

SOCIAL AND EMOTIONAL LEARNING FOR THE REAL WORLD™

Rosen Classroom™

I think I can go across.

I think I can get started.

I think I can use my arms.

I think I can use my legs.

I think I can keep going.

I think I can do it.

Words to Know

arm

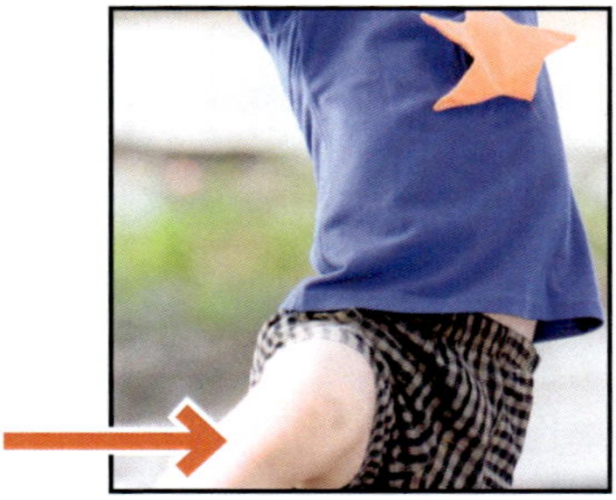

leg